Catnapped

First published in Great Britain 1999 by Mammoth
an imprint of Egmont Children's Books Limited
239 Kensington High Street, London W8 6SA.
Published in hardback by Heinemann Library,
a division of Reed Educational and Professional Publishing Limited
by arrangement with Egmont Children's Books Limited.
Text copyright © Pippa Goodhart 1999
Illustrations copyright © Joanna Harrison 1999
The Author and Illustrator have asserted their moral rights.
Paperback ISBN 0 7497 3111 7
Hardback ISBN 0 431 06190 4
10 9 8 7 6 5 4 3 2 1
A CIP catalogue record for this title
is available from the British Library.
Printed at Oriental Press Limited, Dubai.

Catnapped

Pippa Goodhart

Illustrated by *Joanna Harrison*

 **YELLOW BANANAS**

Chapter One

'ANY MORE IDEAS?' asked Mrs Marsden. 'Any more ideas about living in a way that helps our planet instead of damaging it?'

Ralph's hand shot into the air. 'My cat's a vegetarian!' he said.

'Goodness,' said Mrs Marsden. That wasn't quite the sort of answer she had been expecting.

But for the first time that lesson the class were looking interested. So Mrs Marsden wrote down 'vegetarian cat' on the board above 'insulation', 'recycling' and 'turning off the lights'.

Bethan turned in her chair to face Ralph. 'Wouldn't your cat eat any meat, then?' she asked. 'I mean, what would it do if you waved a mouse under its nose? Would it shake paws and say good morning, or would it bite off the mouse's head like any normal cat would?'

Ralph pushed his glasses up his nose and thought fast. Velvet, his cat, didn't actually eat very much at all. Ralph thought that must be because vegetarian food was more nourishing than meat. He'd never tried him with a mouse and he never would.

'He only ever eats cheese and vegetables and bread and Marmite,' he told Bethan, and that was true.

'Can we test it?' asked Bethan. 'Please, Mrs Marsden? It'd be really interesting!'

'Yes!' said Ralph. 'Please let's!' This was his chance to show the children in his class that life could be lived without eating meat and killing animals. Ralph looked eagerly towards Bethan.

'Come to my house and I'll show you my cat eating vegetables. Then you can tell the others!'

Bethan didn't look impressed. 'I bet you just make it eat those things,' she said. 'It's natural for cats to hunt and eat meat, isn't it?'

Mrs Marsden thought the same. Her cat certainly ate meat, even if it was only meat that came out of tins.

'But my cat does hunt!' said Ralph. 'He hunts plants. I've seen him jumping on the asparagus and nibbling it in our vegetable patch!'

Bethan laughed. 'That's not hunting!' she said. 'Asparagus doesn't run, does it?'

'He chases runner beans too,' said Ralph. His ears went pink and he smiled when everyone laughed.

'Well, you should see my cat,' said Bethan. 'He does it properly. You know, stalking, pouncing, all that. And he eats what he catches. We hardly ever have to buy him tins of cat food, so . . . ' Bethan shot a glance towards Mrs Marsden, '. . . that saves on unnecessary packaging. And he's environmentally friendly

because he kills off mice that would eat
farmers' crops, and rats that spread diseases.
He stays out all night, hunting. He even caught
a weasel once and they're ever so fierce. He
even . . .'

'Yes, Bethan, I think we've got the point.
Now, can we please think about insulation,'
said Mrs Marsden. 'Has anybody got anything

to say?' Nobody had. The class slumped
back onto their chairs and waited for Mrs
Marsden to provide her own answers.
But a note was passed along the tables
from Ralph to Bethan.

It said:

> Come to my house
> tomorrow morning.
> I'll show you my cat
> and then you'll
> believe me.
> Ralph

Bethan read the note. Then she turned to
Ralph and gave him a thumbs-up sign.

Chapter Two

MRS MARSDEN READ poetry with them after lunch. She put on her poetry voice and whispered loudly:

> 'Tyger! Tyger! Burning bright
> In the forests of the night . . .'*

The next bit didn't make sense and Ralph stopped listening. But thinking about tigers made him think about cats and thinking about cats made him think about Velvet.

*'*The Tyger*' by William Blake

Velvet was Ralph's best friend, but, more than that, he was his inspiration. The arrival of Velvet had started Ralph on his Great Plan. Ever since he was tiny, Ralph cared very much about animals. His parents were busy people. He had no brothers or sisters to play with so he had to make friends with the small creatures in his garden. And then one wonderful day his mother had said to him, 'Dad and I have been wondering, would you like to have a proper pet?'

They had been surprised when Ralph had said 'no thank you' to a puppy. He didn't want to pull any animal around by its neck. He had said 'no' to a guinea pig too. He didn't want to shut any animal into a cage. But there was one sort of pet that could stay free. A cat could be a good companion, but still go when and where it liked.

'Can I have a cat, please?' Ralph had asked. There was still a problem with a cat, though, and it worried Ralph. He couldn't bear the thought of his cat killing birds and mice and then eating them. He knew that he would have to find himself an exceptional cat, a cat that wouldn't hunt and wouldn't eat meat.

At the Cats' Home Ralph had known instantly which one was the exceptional kitten that he was looking for. He had picked out the spiky, squeaking, green-eyed ball of black fluff that was little Velvet. 'I want this one, please,' he had told the lady.

In the car on the way home, Ralph had taken a small wrapped lump of cheese out of his

pocket. He had unwrapped the cheese and
held it in front of the kitten's startled face. The
kitten had sniffed and sneezed and then licked
at the cheese with a bright pink tongue that
flickered out and then in again very fast.

'Go on!' Ralph had encouraged, and a
moment later the kitten had sunk his little
pointy fangs into the cheese and gobbled
it all up. 'I knew it!' Ralph had told one tiny
tufted triangle of ear. 'You do eat cheese!'

'What are you doing with that cat?' his father
had asked over his shoulder from the driver's

seat. Ralph was already thinking up his Great Plan.

Ralph's thoughts had gone like this: if a cat would eat cheese instead of eating a mouse that eats the cheese, then perhaps lions would eat grass instead of eating the gazelles that feed on grass. Perhaps crocodiles would eat water weed?

Perhaps . . .

These days Ralph thought about his Great Plan every morning before he got out of bed. He always woke to feel the comforting warm heaviness of Velvet on his feet, and he thought his best Great Plan thoughts as Velvet went through his morning ritual of stretching  and cleaning. Ralph told Velvet about his latest thoughts and Velvet purred in agreement.

'Ralph?' Mrs Marsden's voice calling his name jolted Ralph away from his thoughts and back to the classroom. 'What word might you choose to describe a cat?' she asked him.

'Brilliant!' said Ralph, and Mrs Marsden added 'brilliant' to 'soft', 'cuddly' and 'flowing' that were already on the board.

Bethan caught hold of Ralph's arm as they left the classroom. 'What shall I bring tomorrow?' she asked. 'I might be able to find a mouse or I could look for a tin of tuna in the cupboard?'

'No,' said Ralph. 'I don't want any dead animals. I'll just show you how Velvet eats cheese and things and then you'll see that cats can be vegetarian. You'd better come early, about 7 o'clock, because Velvet goes out later on and we couldn't be sure of finding him.'

Bethan hesitated. She had wanted to find out

if Ralph's cat would refuse meat, but she could see that Ralph wouldn't let her do a test like that. Perhaps she could hide a bit of meat in her pocket? Ralph needn't know and she could watch to see the cat's reaction to the smell of the meat.

'All right,' she agreed. 'But only if you come over to my house afterwards and see if you can get my cat to eat cheese too.'

'OK,' said Ralph, glad that Bethan hadn't insisted on bringing meat.

Chapter Three

ON THE WAY home from school Bethan
thought about tomorrow. She would enjoy
showing Ralph how wild and beautiful her cat,
Panther, was. Then he'll see how natural it is
for a cat to hunt, she thought. He'll see how it
makes an animal free from depending on
people. Panther's independence was the thing
that she admired and loved most about him.

It was one of those damp autumn afternoons
when the light goes early and people hurry to
shut themselves into cars and houses. But

Bethan didn't want to shut herself anywhere. She loved the freedom of this in-between time. The noise and bustle of school had finished, and the noise and bustle of home hadn't quite begun. Two of Bethan's brothers, Tom and Danny, were on the pavement in front of her. They were arguing about something and swinging school bags at each other. Bethan didn't want to be inside her house with their noisy argument.

She glanced over her shoulder to make sure
that her other brother, John, and her sister, Jess,
were not yet on their way home from school.
Then she clambered over the tatty wooden
fence into the garden.

'Panther!' she called quietly. 'Panther!'

Bethan's garden was like a mini jungle. It was
a tangled mix of long grasses and old trees.

Mum hated the garden at this time of year when the trees dropped their leaves and nobody found time to rake them up, but Bethan loved it. You could walk more quietly on soggy layers of leaves than you could on crisp dry ones. And at this dusk time of day you could be invisible as well as silent.

Bethan even loved the sound of the word 'dusk', although she would never admit that to anyone, least of all to Mrs Marsden in a poetry lesson. Dusk is that magical time when lights are turned on inside homes, but the people inside can only see darkness when they look out. And dusk was Panther's time to be in the garden. Panther was as black as the cupboard under the stairs at midnight. He stalked silently through the garden, afraid of nothing. Birds and mice cowered or fled if they sensed that he was near, but Bethan called him to her. She felt powerful when he was with her, a bit like a witch.

Panther first came to Bethan a long time ago
when she had run away from home. Her
brother Danny had taken her sister Jess's watch
without asking and Jess had accused Bethan of
taking it when she hadn't. Mum, as usual, had
listened to Jess and not to Bethan. Danny
hadn't owned up, and so Bethan had been sent
to her room when she hadn't done anything
wrong. That was why she had run away. She

had run as far as the garden. Then, in the garden, she had discovered two things that stopped her from running any further. She had discovered the magic of the garden at dusk and she had discovered Panther.

Now, as she called his name again, Panther was suddenly there, galloping silently over the fallen leaves and coming to wind himself around her legs and push his cheek against her knee.

Bethan sat down on a damp log so that Panther could jump onto her lap. His body rattled with purrs as she stroked a finger down his spine. He rubbed the hard silky top of his head on the underside of Bethan's chin.

Bethan tipped her head on one side so that her cheek could rest on its softness. That first time that Panther had come to her, he had suddenly appeared darkly out of a shadowy tree and demanded attention and fuss, just as he was doing now.

Since then, Panther had become part of Bethan's family. If it was cold outside and he fancied a soft warm chair, then in Panther came. If a quarrel started or the television was on too loud, then out he went.

'He's his own cat,' Bethan's dad always said. Bethan wished that she could be like that, brave and independent. Looking at Panther now, Bethan laughed.

'You're not going to eat that cheese tomorrow, are you?' The idea seemed ridiculous. 'You're a real cat, not like Ralph's Velvet!'

Panther seemed to grin and he purred and worked his claws, prickling through Bethan's school skirt to her leg.

'Ow!' she protested, and Panther leapt away into the dark shadows of the garden.

He had gone again.

Chapter Four

'COME IN,' RALPH told Bethan as he opened the door next morning. Bethan paused in the doorway and gazed at the inside of Ralph's house. She had never seen so many books before. 'Have you got any books about wild animals?' she asked.

Ralph nodded. 'Yes, loads. Come on. Velvet's waiting in the kitchen for his breakfast. I've got it all ready.'

Bethan was wondering if she dare ask to borrow one of the books as she followed Ralph into the kitchen.

'This is Velvet,' said Ralph, and he pointed proudly towards a rocking chair. A sleek black cat uncurled itself from the patchwork cushioned seat, stretched up onto its toes and yawned a large toothy yawn. Bethan knew that yawn, and she knew the cunning green eyes that gleamed above it.

'No it isn't!' she said.

Ralph pushed his glasses up his nose. 'What do you mean, "no it isn't"?' He scooped the purring cat into his arms and began to stroke him.

Bethan felt panic churning inside her. The Marmite and crackers, the cheese and the crisps in their neat row of bowls on the table were forgotten. 'He's mine! He's Panther!' Bethan cradled the cat, and the cat went on purring as though he really did love her.

Ralph felt desperate. 'He's in my kitchen because he lives here! He's always been mine!

I chose him when he was a tiny kitten!'

'Well,' said Bethan, 'you might have chosen him, but he chose me! He must have got tired of boring old cheese and boring old you because he came and found me ages ago. This is definitely Panther!'

It felt to Ralph as though somebody had punched him in the chest at the same time as opening a trapdoor under his feet. Could Velvet really love somebody else, belong to somebody else? Could Velvet, the vegetarian cat, also be Panther the great hunter?

'No!' said Ralph, and he reached out to pull Velvet out of Bethan's arms. He pulled hard and Bethan pulled back. The cat growled and hissed and sprang out of their tangle of arms and shot off through the cat-flap into the garden.

'Velvet!' called Ralph.

'Panther!' called Bethan, but the cat-flap clattered shut. Bethan turned and looked at Ralph's white face.

'He really was my Panther,' she said.

'We hurt him!' said Ralph. He looked down in disbelief at his empty arms. 'I hurt him!'

Bethan saw Ralph's eyes going watery. 'I'm sure he'll come back,' she said.

Ralph adjusted his glasses and gave his eyes a secret wipe. 'Come on,' he said. 'Let's find him and he can decide whose he is.' Then Ralph remembered that he didn't believe in owning animals. 'I mean who he is, not whose,' he corrected himself.

Together Ralph and Bethan went into Ralph's neat garden and together they looked for the sleek black cat.

I must let him choose whichever one of us he wants, Ralph told himself, but his chest ached inside.

Together they searched the jungle that was Bethan's garden. Bethan chewed her cheek

inside her mouth. Of course Panther was free
to go where he liked. That was the wonderful
thing about him. But she couldn't help
wondering why he had come and made her
love him if he already loved somebody else?

'Shall we look down the road?' Bethan asked,
and Ralph nodded. Side by side, in unspoken
agreement that neither should go in front or
behind, they walked along the pavement and
looked over into all the gardens as they went.

'Panther!' 'Velvet!' they called, but no black
cat came running to greet them. Somebody
noticed them though.

'Hello, you two!' said Mrs Marsden from her
garden. 'Have you lost something?'

Stalking down the path behind
her ambled a sleek black cat
with a grin on its face.

Chapter Five

'PANTHER!' SAID BETHAN.

'Velvet!' said Ralph, and they both rushed to claim the cat.

With unhurried grace the cat leapt up onto the garden wall, just out of reach. It settled down to snooze in the morning sun.

Mrs Marsden looked startled. 'No,' she said. 'I call my cat Solomon.'

'But . . .' began Bethan and Ralph, and, both

talking at once, they explained about Panther and Velvet.

'Oh, I see,' said Mrs Marsden, her heart beating suddenly rather fast. 'Are you sure that this is the same cat? There are lots of black cats, you know.'

They looked at the cat on the wall. It opened one eye and seemed to grin back.

'Yes,' said Bethan. 'But how can he be yours too?'

'Well,' said Mrs Marsden. 'He isn't with me all the time. Usually he comes at night and keeps me company before I go to bed. And he often comes again at lunch time for his tin of food.' Then Mrs Marsden smiled. 'My goodness, do you both feed him too? It's a wonder he isn't as round as a barrel!'

Panther Velvet Solomon grinned and sat up. He poked one back leg straight up in the air and began to lick it.

'He's mine,' said Bethan quietly but firmly, and she took a step forward.

Ralph thought of that comforting weight on his feet when he woke each morning. 'No,' he said. 'He's mine. Bethan just catnapped him.'

Ralph grabbed at Bethan's shoulder to stop her going any nearer to the cat. Bethan pulled away and they started to fight.

'Now then, you two!' said Mrs Marsden. 'You are both sensible enough to know that that's no way to settle an argument!'

Ralph stepped back and rearranged his glasses. He'd never hit anyone before. 'What shall we do?' he asked. 'He's sort of yours too, isn't he?'

Mrs Marsden smiled. 'Yes,' she said.

Mrs Marsden had loved and lost people during her lifetime and she told herself that she shouldn't mind too much about a cat. But she did. Her house  always seemed so quiet after the liveliness of the day at school. She looked forward to the arrival of Solomon each evening for a chat before bed.

'Come and sit down,' she told Ralph and Bethan. 'We'll decide what to do.'

They sat down on the garden bench and

watched the cat on the wall while Mrs Marsden
told them about another Solomon, a wise king
in the Bible. 'He had to make a choice too,'
she said. 'Two women came to see King
Solomon. They brought a baby with them and
each woman said that the baby belonged to
her. "Please decide which of us is the true

mother," they asked King Solomon. Well, King Solomon thought for a while, and then he said something rather shocking and very clever. He told the two women, "The only fair way to resolve this is to share the baby between you. We will cut the baby in half and you shall have half each!"

"Never!" shouted one of the women. "Give my baby to the other woman rather than harm him!"

King Solomon smiled when he heard that. "Give the baby to the woman who cried out," he said. "'She loves the child more than herself. She is the true mother.'"

'But that won't work for our cat,' said Bethan. 'None of us would let him be cut up!'

'You're right, of course,' agreed Mrs Marsden.

'That's because we all love and own him at the same time.'

'No,' said Ralph. He could feel a new theory about animals beginning to form in his mind. Perhaps it could turn into a new Great Plan, even a book, some day? 'I think that actually he owns us,' he said, 'not the other way around. He is the one who needs to do the deciding.'

Solomon Velvet Panther yawned an extravagant yawn and jumped down off the wall. He ambled over towards the garden

bench. Bethan, Mrs Marsden and Ralph all held
their breath. Was he about to choose? Which of
their laps would he decide to jump onto? Or
would he wind around the legs of just one of
them?

Velvet Panther
Solomon seemed to
grin from one pointed
ear to the other and
he stopped on the path
an exactly equal distance
from each of the three
of them. Then he sat
down and closed his eyes.
There was a moment of
silence, and then they all
laughed.

'There we are!' said Mrs Marsden. 'He's
chosen us all!'

Bethan turned to Ralph. 'But what about the
test?' she asked. 'Is he vegetarian or is he a
hunter? Or,' she looked at Mrs Marsden, 'is he
an ordinary tinned-food cat?'

44

'I think that he's the one testing us!' said
Ralph. 'He's found out what sort of cat we each
want, and he's been that different sort of cat to
each of us.'

'But I wonder what sort of cat he really is?'
said Bethan. 'Inside himself, I mean.'

Ralph scratched his head and frowned. Mrs Marsden just laughed.

'Who knows!' she said. 'Come inside and I'll get us all a drink.'

The black cat followed them up the path. He seemed to be smiling.

Yellow Bananas are bright, funny, brilliantly imaginative stories written by some of today's top writers. All the books are beautifully illustrated in full colour.

So if you've enjoyed this story, why not pick another from the bunch?